© Flammarion, 2001
87, quai Panhard et Levassor – 75647 Paris Cedex 13
www.editions.flammarion.com
Originally published in French under the title
*Gare à Edgar!*
by Flammarion, 2001
This English language translation © Eerdmans Books for Young Readers

Published in 2015 by Eerdmans Books for Young Readers,
an imprint of Wm. B. Eerdmans Publishing Co.
2140 Oak Industrial Dr. NE
Grand Rapids, Michigan 49505
P.O. Box 163, Cambridge CB3 9PU U.K.

www.eerdmans.com/youngreaders

Manufactured at Tien Wah Press
in Malaysia in August 2014, first printing

21 20 19 18 17 16 15      9 8 7 6 5 4 3 2 1

Library of Congress Cataloging-in-Publication Data

Dumont, Jean-François, author, illustrator.
[Gare à Edgar! English]
Edgar wants to be alone / written and illustrated by Jean-François
Dumont; [translated by Leslie Mathews].
pages cm
Summary: Edgar, a rat who wants nothing more than to be left alone,
spies an earthworm following him about the farm and does everything
he can think of to get rid of it before learning an important lesson.
ISBN 978-0-8028-5457-5
[1. Rats — Fiction. 2. Earthworms — Fiction.] I. Mathews, Leslie,
translator. II. Title.

PZ7.D89367Edg 2015
[E] — dc23

2014018605

For Florence.
— *J. F. D.*

# EDGAR WANTS TO BE ALONE

Written and illustrated by
**JEAN-FRANÇOIS DUMONT**

Eerdmans Books for Young Readers

Grand Rapids, Michigan • Cambridge, U.K.

Edgar the rat was furious. He had been
walking, when suddenly he noticed
that an earthworm was following him.
Edgar tried to surprise it by turning
around, but the wary worm hid behind
him and managed to keep out of sight.

But the worm *was* behind him. Edgar was sure of it.

As soon as he took a step, he heard the worm sliding in the wet grass, and when he stopped, the worm stopped too. A worm having fun following a rat — that wasn't such a big deal — but Edgar was not exactly an ordinary rat.

Edgar lived at the back of the garden, under an old apple tree that provided him with food. He had made a cozy little nest in an abandoned crate. He didn't want company. He lived alone and had forbidden anyone to disturb him.

The other animals had gotten used to his bad temper. They had avoided the back of the garden ever since Edgar bit a rabbit who had come a little too close to his home. Most of the farm animals pretended not to see him when they crossed his path during the day.

But today, an earthworm had made up its mind to ruin the beautiful morning. Edgar didn't want company. He wanted to be alone! He started running around the barn as fast as he could — a worm would never be able to crawl that fast! However, when he stopped, out of breath, and glanced furtively over his shoulder . . . the worm was still there.

Edgar decided to go for a swim in the nearby pond.
"Surely worms don't know how to swim," he said to
himself. "I'll get rid of this nuisance once and for all."

After diving, swimming, and doing a few somersaults in the water, Edgar shook himself off at the edge of the pond.

He turned around slowly and — good grief — the worm had followed him again!

Edgar decided to use any means necessary, so he went to find the mole in the field next to the barn and offered her a deal:

"You must be tired of digging to find your food. I'm going to walk by you, and all you have to do is catch the worm that's following me."

Edgar walked back and forth in front of the mole, who finally got angry: "You should be ashamed for mocking me! There's no one behind you, and I can't feed my family when I'm wasting time like this!"

The mole disappeared into her tunnel, leaving Edgar to face his problem alone. "That mole is totally nearsighted!" he thought, shrugging his shoulders.

Edgar went to find the woodpecker and ask for his help:
"Instead of giving yourself a headache pecking on that
tree trunk, why don't you get rid of this worm that's
been following me since this morning?"

The bird fluttered around Edgar, but quickly got upset
with him: "You deserve a good peck on the snout!
There's nothing behind you!"

And with a flap of his wings, the woodpecker returned to his perch and got back to his work. "Hammering on wood has made that woodpecker go soft in the head," Edgar grumbled as he moved on.

Discouraged, Edgar was headed back to the farm, when he saw the pig wallowing in his pond. "Since it seems that you eat anything and everything, how about you catch this blasted earthworm that's following me and make a snack out of it?"

"Since this morning," the pig replied, "I've seen you turn in circles talking to yourself, run around the barn at top speed, stop dead in your tracks, jump into the water, shake yourself off, and then walk back and forth in front of the mole and the woodpecker. Now you're asking me to eat a worm that doesn't exist. I'm wondering if maybe the sun hasn't given you sunstroke. So put on a hat when you go out for a walk on a sunny day, and meanwhile, go home and get some rest."

With that the pig closed his eyes . . . and went back to sleep.

"All of those days spent sleeping in the mud haven't done *him* any good," Edgar sighed to himself. "It must have affected his eyes."

The running around, the swimming, and all of the annoyances *had* worn him out, so Edgar decided to take the pig's advice.

He was comfortably settled in bed when, all of a sudden, between his feet, he saw a bit of the earthworm. The worm, not content to follow him all day long, apparently had decided to sleep in his bed!

Infuriated, Edgar didn't hesitate, and bit down hard on it.

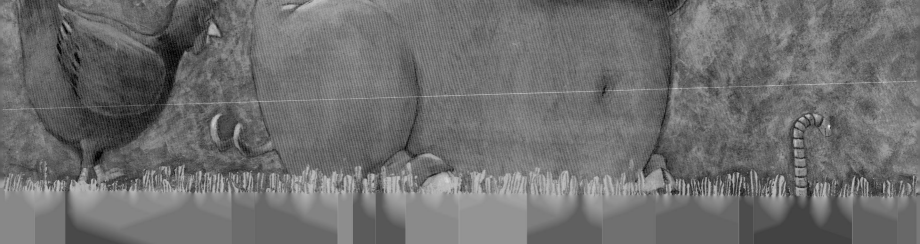

Ever since that day, all of the animals on the farm laugh when they tell the story of Edgar, the rat who mistook his tail for a worm.

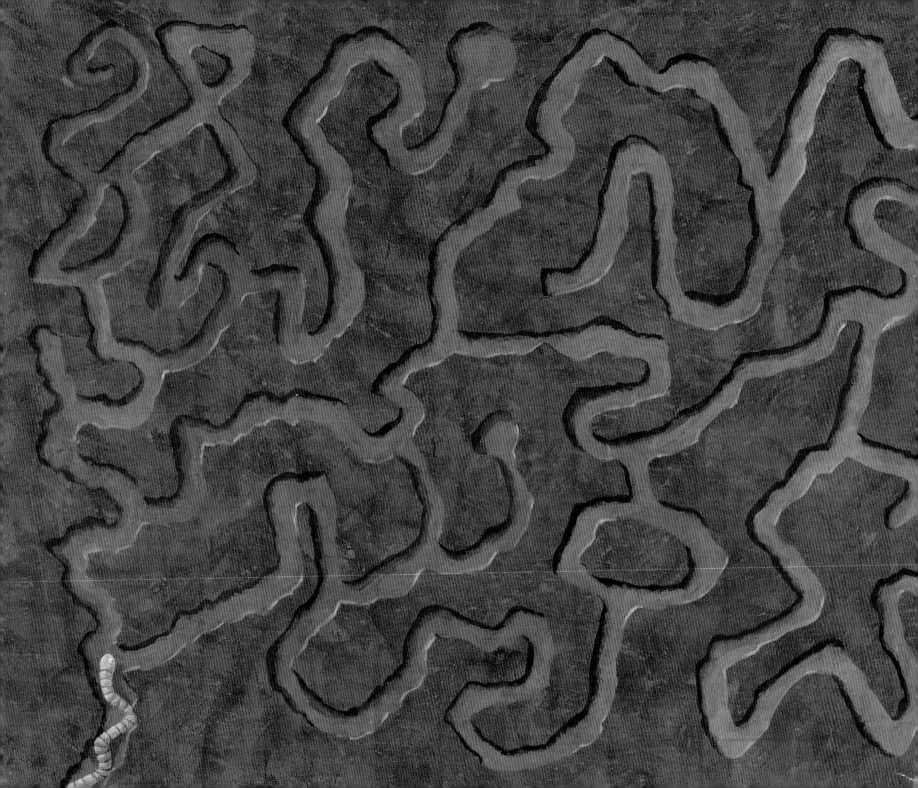